This Little Tiger book belongs to:

_____

_____

_____

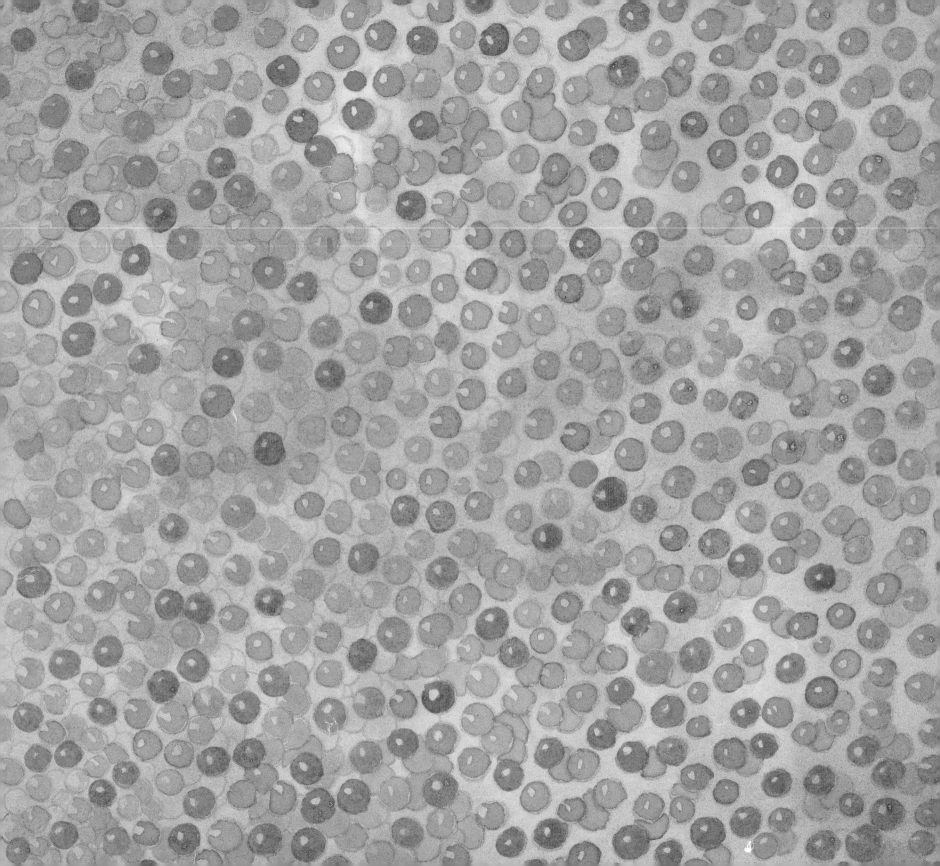

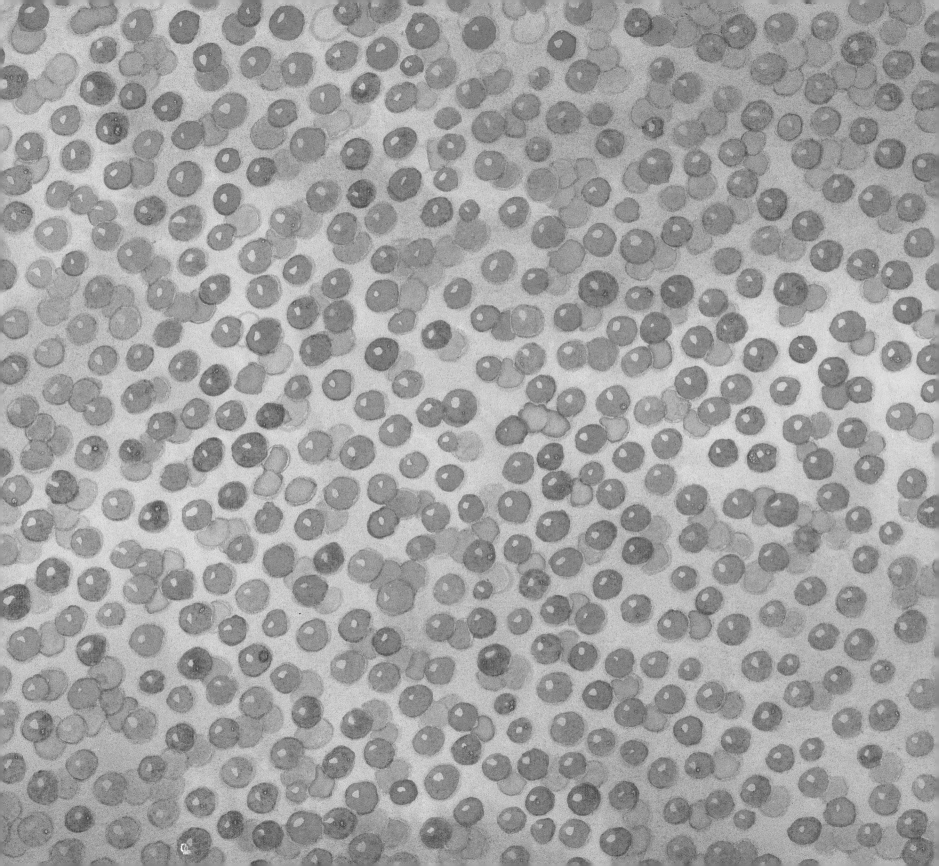

To my dad and his 'Bangy' peas – S S

To David, my King Full of Beans – J D

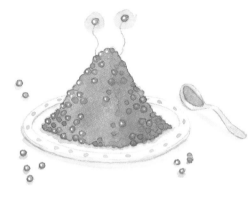

LITTLE TIGER PRESS
An imprint of Magi Publications
1 The Coda Centre, 189 Munster Road, London SW6 6AW
www.littletigerpress.com

First published in Great Britain 2008
This edition published 2009

A CIP catalogue record for this book is available from the British Library

Printed in Singapore

10 9 8 7 6 5 4 3 2 1

Smelly Peter
The Great Pea Eater

Steve Smallman

Joelle Dreidemy

LITTLE TIGER PRESS
London

Young Peter Pod was a little bit odd:
he ate nothing but peas, fresh or tinned,
For breakfast and brunch, for dinner and lunch,
though he always had terrible wind!

Then early one morning,
without any warning,
Peter turned green as a pea.

Petit Pois

trump

parp

School

He thought he looked cool,
and he rushed off to school,
so that all of his class mates
could see.

But kids like to tease
boys the colour of peas.
They were rotten
to Peter all day.

At the back of the class,
in a cloud of green gas,
Peter thought about
running away.

That night, after dark, Peter ran to the park.

The stars were all twinkly and bright.

He saw a strange glow, then a big U.F.O.

came and whisked him off into the night.

Some little green men stared at Peter and then, they knelt down and started to sing,
"You're the loveliest **green** that we have ever seen, oh, please say you'll be our new **king!**"

Peter agreed, so they shot off at speed
to the planet of Krell, far away.

Then they asked if King Pete
would like something to eat
and he said,
"I'll have **peas**, if I may."

"What's a **pea?**"

asked the cooks and exchanged worried looks
for they'd made him a Krellian pie,
Plus a wonderful feast, so that Peter at least
had to give *half* the dishes a try.

The food was all right! Peter **trumped** with delight!

Then they all had a marvellous party.

And the funny thing was, they all loved him because

he was green and incredibly farty!

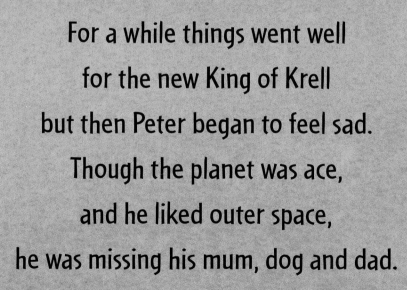

For a while things went well
for the new King of Krell
but then Peter began to feel sad.
Though the planet was ace,
and he liked outer space,
he was missing his mum, dog and dad.

Then Peter turned **PINK!**

(lack of peas do you think?)

which upset all the people of Krell.

They had wanted a lovely,

green, trumpety king.

Now he'd even stopped trumping as well!

They took off his crown
and his velvety gown.
There were angry green
faces all round him.

Boot!

Then without a farewell,
the ex-King of Krell
was dumped back on the earth
where they'd found him.

"Hey, look it's our Peter.
He's pink and smells sweeter!
And he's hungry.
We know what that means . . ."

But Peter said, "Please!
Don't give me those peas!
From now on I just want . . ."

"BAKED BEANS!"

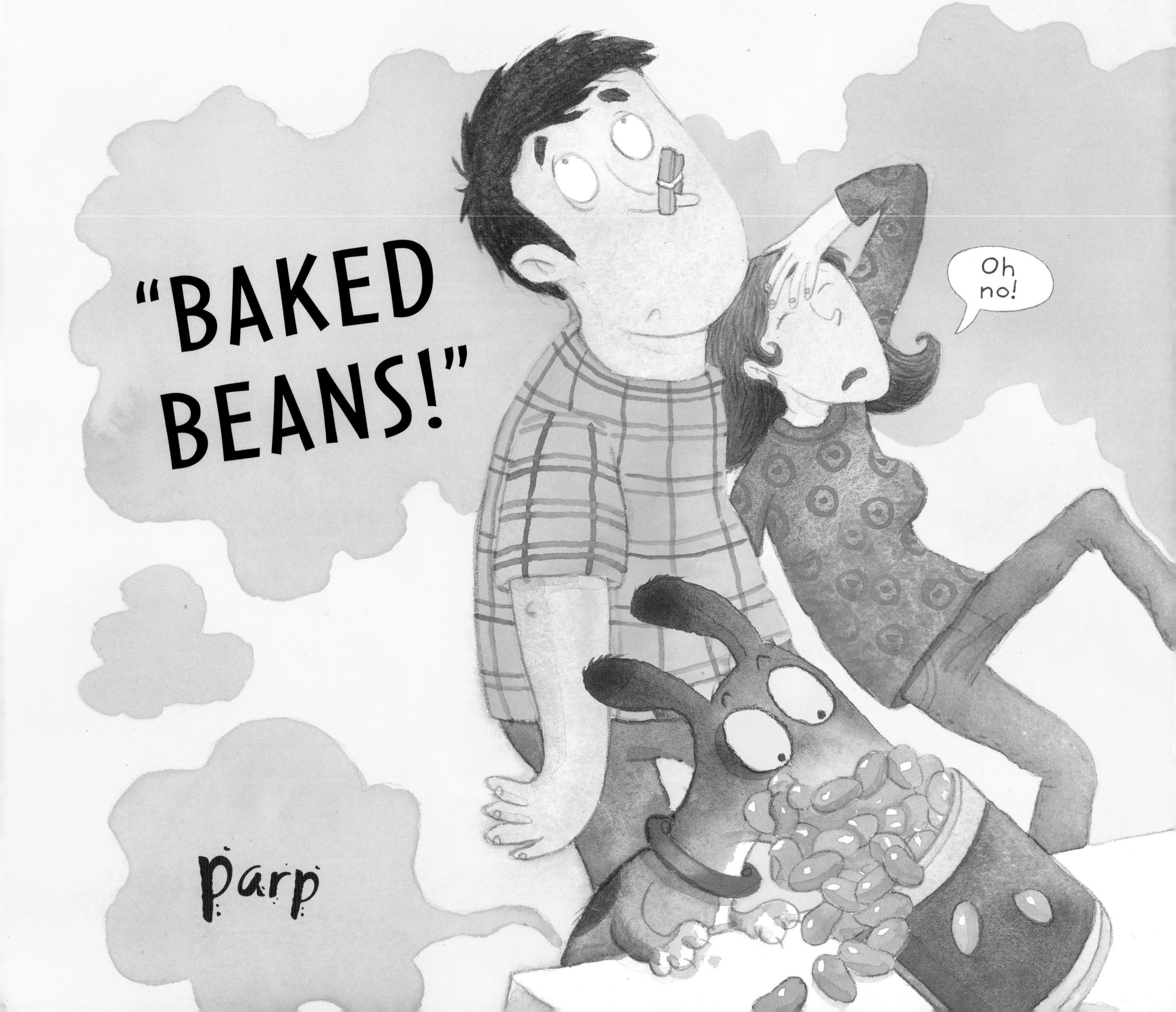